MW01493780

Arctic Animals

by Elizabeth Neuenfeldt

BELLWETHER MEDIA • MINNEAPOLIS, MN

BLASTOFF!
2
READERS

Blastoff! Readers are carefully developed by literacy experts to build reading stamina and move students toward fluency by combining standards-based content with developmentally appropriate text.

Level 1 provides the most support through repetition of high-frequency words, light text, predictable sentence patterns, and strong visual support.

Level 2 offers early readers a bit more challenge through varied sentences, increased text load, and text-supportive special features.

Level 3 advances early-fluent readers toward fluency through increased text load, less reliance on photos, advancing concepts, longer sentences, and more complex special features.

★ **Blastoff! Universe**

Reading Level

Grade
K

Grades
1–3

Grade
4

This edition first published in 2023 by Bellwether Media, Inc.

No part of this publication may be reproduced in whole or in part without written permission of the publisher. For information regarding permission, write to Bellwether Media, Inc., Attention: Permissions Department, 6012 Blue Circle Drive, Minnetonka, MN 55343.

Library of Congress Cataloging-in-Publication Data

LC record for Arctic Animals available at: https://lccn.loc.gov/2022009378

Text copyright © 2023 by Bellwether Media, Inc. BLASTOFF! READERS and associated logos are trademarks and/or registered trademarks of Bellwether Media, Inc.

Editor: Rachael Barnes   Designer: Brittany McIntosh

Printed in the United States of America, North Mankato, MN.

Table of Contents

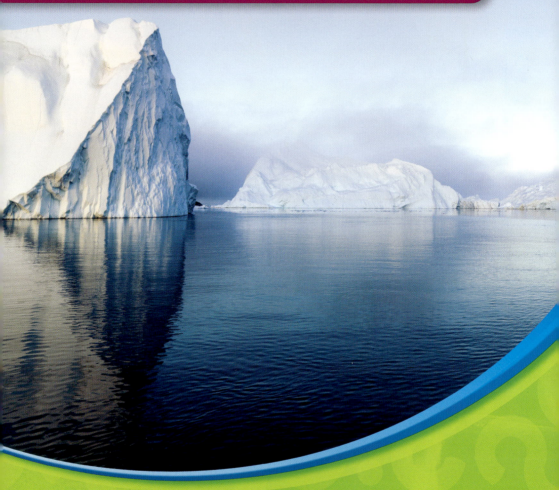

The Arctic is in the northernmost part of the earth. This **biome** is often cold and icy.

4

Many animals have **adapted** to the Arctic seasons!

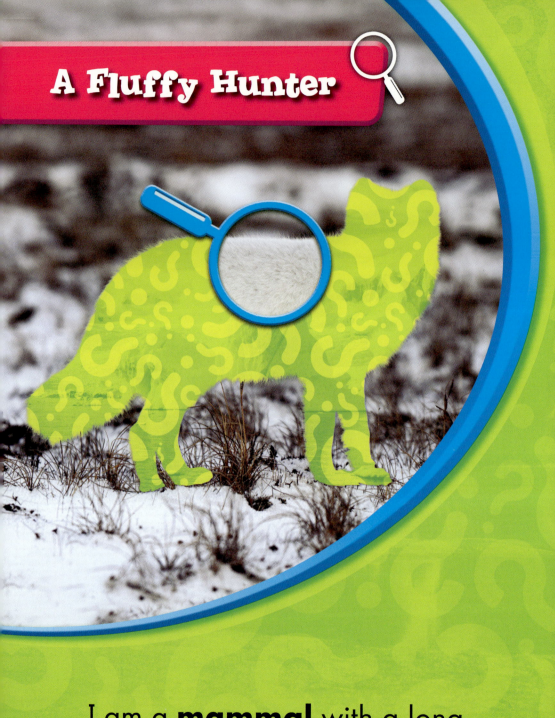

I am a **mammal** with a long, fluffy tail.

I run quietly over ice and snow with my padded paws. What animal am I?

More About Me!

range =

| Least Concern | Near Threatened | Vulnerable | Endangered | Critically Endangered | Extinct in the Wild | Extinct |

conservation status: least concern

life span: 3 to 6 years

class: mammal

how I stand out:

long, fluffy tail

padded paws

I am an Arctic fox!
I live in **dens** with
other Arctic foxes.

I am an **omnivore**.
My sharp claws
help me dig for food!

den

Arctic Fox Food

lemmings   seals   berries

I am a mammal with **flippers** and **whiskers**.

I swim in cold oceans and move slowly on land. What animal am I?

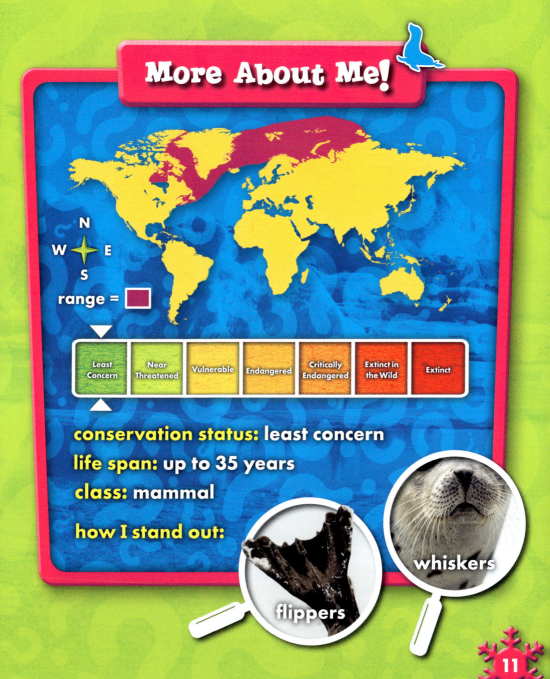

N
W E
S

range = ▇

Least Concern	Near Threatened	Vulnerable	Endangered	Critically Endangered	Extinct in the Wild	Extinct

conservation status: least concern

life span: up to 35 years

class: mammal

how I stand out:

flippers

whiskers

11

Harp Seal Food

fish   shrimp   krill

I am a harp seal!
I hunt for fish
and **crustaceans**
underwater.

My whiskers
help me find food
while I swim!

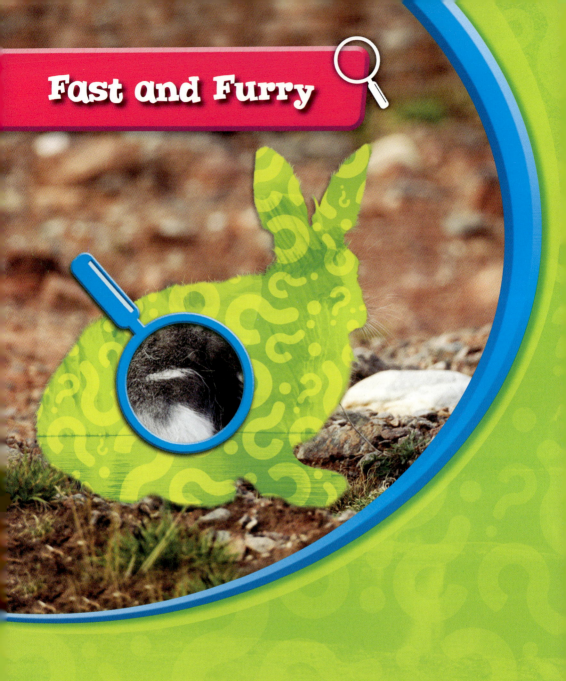

I am a small, furry mammal.
My fur changes color with
the seasons. It hides me.

14

My strong legs help me hop quickly out of danger! What animal am I?

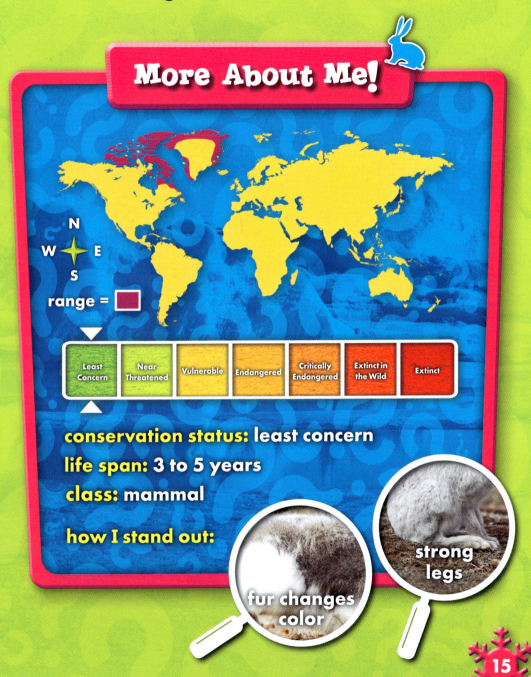

More About Me!

N W E S

range = ■

Least Concern	Near Threatened	Vulnerable	Endangered	Critically Endangered	Extinct in the Wild	Extinct

conservation status: least concern

life span: 3 to 5 years

class: mammal

how I stand out:

fur changes color

strong legs

I am an Arctic hare!
I am **nocturnal**.

I mostly eat plants.
My sharp claws
dig through deep snow
to reach food.

Arctic Hare Food

berries   moss   leaves

17

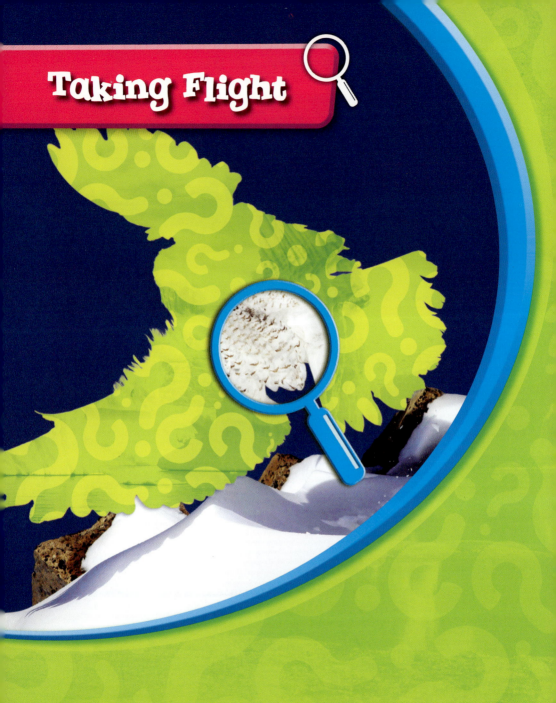

I am a bird with white feathers and huge wings.

I have round, yellow eyes and sharp **talons**. What animal am I?

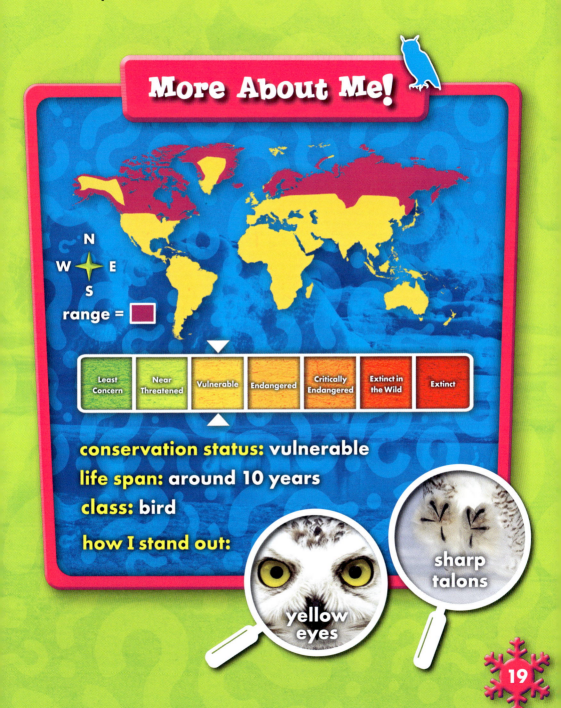

More About Me!

N
W E
S

range = ▮

| Least Concern | Near Threatened | Vulnerable | Endangered | Critically Endangered | Extinct in the Wild | Extinct |

conservation status: vulnerable

life span: around 10 years

class: bird

how I stand out:

yellow eyes

sharp talons

Snowy Owl Food

geese   lemmings   hares

I am a snowy owl!
I am a **carnivore**
with excellent hearing.
I can hear **prey**
hiding in the snow.

I am one of many
outstanding animals
in the Arctic!

Glossary

adapted—changed over a long period of time

biome—a large area with certain plants, animals, and weather

carnivore—an animal that only eats meat

crustaceans—animals that have several pairs of legs and hard outer shells; crabs and shrimp are types of crustaceans.

dens—sheltered places

flippers—wide, flat body parts that are used for swimming

mammal—a warm-blooded animal that has a backbone and feeds its young milk

nocturnal—active at night

omnivore—an animal that eats both plants and animals

prey—animals that are hunted by other animals for food

talons—sharp claws on birds that allow them to grab and tear into their food

whiskers—long hairs growing near an animal's mouth

To Learn More

AT THE LIBRARY

Kingsley, Imogen. *An Arctic Food Web*. Mankato, Minn.: Amicus, 2021.

Rustad, Martha E.H. *Animals of the Arctic Tundra*. North Mankato, Minn.: Capstone Press, 2022.

Stratton, Connor. *Life in the Arctic*. Mendota Heights, Minn.: Little Blue House, 2020.

ON THE WEB

FACTSURFER

Factsurfer.com gives you a safe, fun way to find more information.

1. Go to www.factsurfer.com.

2. Enter "Arctic animals" into the search box and click 🔍.

3. Select your book cover to see a list of related content.

Index

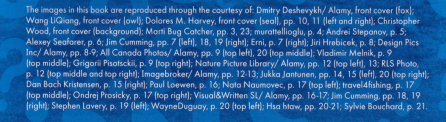

The images in this book are reproduced through the courtesy of: Dmitry Deshevykh/ Alamy, front cover (fox); Wang LiQiang, front cover (owl); Dolores M. Harvey, front cover (seal), pp. 10, 11 (left and right); Christopher Wood, front cover (background); Marti Bug Catcher, pp. 3, 23; murattellioglu, p. 4; Andrei Stepanov, p. 5; Alexey Seafarer, p. 6; Jim Cumming, pp. 7 (left), 18, 19 (right); Erni, p. 7 (right); Jiri Hrebicek, p. 8; Design Pics Inc/ Alamy, pp. 8-9; All Canada Photos/ Alamy, pp. 9 (top left), 20 (top middle); Vladimir Melnik, p. 9 (top middle); Grigorii Pisotskii, p. 9 (top right); Nature Picture Library/ Alamy, pp. 12 (top left), 13; RLS Photo, p. 12 (top middle and top right); Imagebroker/ Alamy, pp. 12-13; Jukka Jantunen, pp. 14, 15 (left), 20 (top right); Dan Bach Kristensen, p. 15 (right); Paul Loewen, p. 16; Nata Naumovec, p. 17 (top left); travel4fishing, p. 17 (top middle); Ondrej Prosicky, p. 17 (top right); Visual&Written SL/ Alamy, pp. 16-17; Jim Cumming, pp. 18, 19 (right); Stephen Lavery, p. 19 (left); WayneDuguay, p. 20 (top left); Hsa htaw, pp. 20-21; Sylvie Bouchard, p. 21.